MAGIC BONE

NICE SNOWING YOU!

GROSSET & DUNLAP
Published by the Penguin Group
Penguin Group (USA) LLC, 375 Hudson Street, New York, New York 10014, USA

USA | Canada | UK | Ireland | Australia | New Zealand | India | South Africa | China

penguin.com
A Penguin Random House Company

Library of Congress Cataloging-in-Publication Data is available.

ISBN 978-0-448-46446-6   10 9 8 7 6 5 4 3 2 1

MAGIC BONE

NICE SNOWING YOU!

by Nancy Krulik
illustrated by Sebastien Braun

Grosset & Dunlap
An Imprint of Penguin Group (USA) LLC

For Gladys and Steve Krulik, Josie's
favorite puppy-sitters—NK

For Leo and Archie—SB

CHAPTER 1

"Queenie, get out of my yard!" I bark as loud as I can. I'm trying to scare that mean old cat away.

Queenie doesn't budge. She just sits there under my tree, licking her paws.

"I'm gonna get you!" I bark at her.

Queenie yawns.

Okay. That's it. I warned her. *Wiggle, waggle, whoa!* Here I come!

I start to run after Queenie. But I'm not very fast. It's hard to run with a coat tied around your belly and booties strapped to your paws.

I keep running. Fast. Faster . . . I can't go *fastest*.

Queenie leaps up onto my fence and laughs at me. I don't speak cat. But I can tell when I'm being laughed at.

"Ha-ha-ha-ha!"

Queenie's not the only one laughing. *That* laugh is coming from the yard next to mine. It's Frankie, the German shepherd who lives next door.

"Nice coat, Sparky," Frankie says. But it sounds like he doesn't really mean it. "You look like a giant red sausage with a head and legs."

"I didn't want to wear a coat," I bark back. "My two-leg, Josh, made me."

"You look ridiculous." Frankie laughs again. "Dogs don't need coats. We already have *fur* coats."

I don't like being laughed at. I'm taking this coat off right now!

I grab the coat with my teeth. *Rip!*

Rip! Rip! My teeth are strong. Pieces of my coat fall to the ground.

Riiiiipppp! I tear at the spot on my coat where the two sides meet. The coat opens. I feel better already.

Shakity, shake, shake! I shake that coat right off.

"Uh-oh, pup," Samson, the old mixed-breed who lives on the other side of the fence, says to me. "Your two-leg gave you that coat to keep you warm. It's a cold day. You shouldn't listen to Frankie. Sometimes he's just teasing you. And that's not nice of him."

"Hey!" Frankie says. "I'm a nice dog. I just—"

Samson doesn't let him finish. "Stop trying to make the pup feel bad about himself," he tells Frankie. "Sparky's two-leg loves him. That's why he gave him that coat."

It feels good to have a smart dog like Samson sticking up for me. But it doesn't feel good not having my coat. It's really cold out here.

I look up at the sky. White stuff is starting to fall on me. It looks like white kibble. I wonder if it tastes like kibble.

"I'm gonna catch you!" I bark to the white stuff. My eyes stare at a piece of fluffy white kibble falling from the sky. I open my mouth and chase it as it falls.

Bang! Ouch! I'm so busy staring up at the white kibble, I don't see my tree standing there.

"Ha-ha!" Frankie starts laughing at me all over again.

Grrrr.

I try to ignore Frankie. So I look down to find the piece of white kibble I was chasing. But I can't see it anymore. It's all mushed up on the ground with the rest of the cold white stuff.

I lower my head and take a bite. *Wiggle, waggle, weird.* This isn't like the kibble in my food bowl. It's more like the water in my water bowl. Only colder. A *lot* colder.

Now my outsides *and* my insides are cold.

I know what will cheer me up! I pad over to my favorite digging spot near the flowers. Or at least where the flowers used to be, before it got so cold. Then I start to dig. *Diggety, dig, di—*

Oh no! I can't dig. The booties are covering my paws. What's a dog to do without his paws?

I lie down and grab one of the booties in my teeth.

Rrrip! The first bootie comes off.

Rrrip! There goes the second.

The booties on my back paws are harder to get to. I reach my head around. I twist my middle. Yes! I've got a bootie in my teeth. *Yank, yank. Rrrip! Rrrip!*

And now the other one. *Yank, yank. Rrrip! Rrrip!*

Whoopee! I'm bootie-free!

Diggety, dig, dig.

The ground is cold and really, really hard. But I'm not giving up. *Diggety, dig, di—*

Sniffety, sniff, sniff, sniff. I smell something really good. Like chicken, beef, and sausage all rolled into one.

The smell is coming from the hole.

I look down. My bone! Right where I left it!

"Hello, bone!" I bark excitedly. Then I stop barking. I don't want Frankie, or even Samson, to know about my bone. This isn't just any bone. It has magic powers. It can *kaboom* me right out of my yard! No, really. The first time I took a big bite of my magic bone, it sent me all the way to London!

London was fun—and yummy. You wouldn't believe the snacks  the two-legs leave on the floor for dogs like me. Sausages, cheese, and fish and chips (that's what the dogs in London call french fries). But London was scary, too. Mean two-legs lived there, such as the dogcatcher, who threw me in the pound, and the Bulldog Boys, who tried to keep all the food for themselves.

Another time I chomped on my bone, I ended up in Hawaii. Did you know that in Hawaii two-legs stand on the water and ride the waves? I don't know why they think it's fun. The giant water bowl there—the two-legs call it the Pacific Ocean—is cold and salty. And the waves are so high that one almost swallowed up my friend Lolani. She was lucky I was there to save her.

But the scariest time came when

my bone *kaboomed* me right into the Land of Cats! Well, it was actually a city in Italy called Rome, but lots of mean cats lived there. Two of them stole my bone. Luckily, the magic only works for dogs, so those cats thought it was just a yummy-smelling bone, nothing more. With the help of my friend Bernardo, I tricked those cats into giving me back my bone, and I made it home again, safe and sound.

Sniffety, sniff, sniff. My magic bone smells so meaty. If I bite into my bone again, I will wind up somewhere else. Somewhere new. Somewhere far, far away. Maybe my bone could take me someplace warm.

Yes, someplace warm would be nice.

Chomp!

Wiggle, waggle, whew! I feel dizzy—like my insides are spinning all around—but my outsides are standing still. Stars are twinkling in front of my eyes—even though it's daytime! All around me I smell food— fried chicken, salmon, roast beef. But there isn't any food in sight.

Kaboom! Kaboom! Kaboom!

CHAPTER 2

The *kabooming* stops. Just like that. The loud scary noise is gone.

But I'm still cold. Really cold. My body is *shakity, shake, shaking.* And my teeth are *chomp, chomp, chomping*—even though there's no food in my mouth for them to chomp on.

There is a lot of white kibble here. Piles and piles of it. The white kibble is as cold here as it was at home. I wonder where *here* is. I've never seen any place like this before.

Sniffety, sniff, sniff. I've never *smelled* any place like it before, either. There's a sweet smell in the air. I think it's coming from those green trees. But that's all I smell. I don't smell other dogs. Or two-legs. Or anyone.

Wiggle, waggle, uh-oh. Am I the only one in this strange place?

Wait a minute. What's that? Over there, by that sweet-smelling tree? It looks like a two-leg. He has eyes, a long nose, and a smiling mouth. And he stands up tall like a two-leg. Only . . .

This two-leg doesn't *have* legs. Just a big round belly and a head.

I clutch my bone tight in my teeth—just in case the two-leg with no legs wants to steal it. But the two-leg with no legs doesn't try to steal my bone. He doesn't move at all.

I sniff his butt. At least I think it's his butt. It's hard to tell. He doesn't smell like a two-leg.

I don't think this two-leg will steal my bone. I don't think he *can*. He has no paws. And he's standing very, very still. Sort of like those statues I saw in Rome.

Diggety, dig, dig. I think I will hide my magic bone right here, near the sweet-smelling trees and the two-leg with no legs. That way I will know just where to find it when I'm ready to go home. I paw my way through the cold, wet white stuff and down to the hard dirt below. I make sure the hole is deep, deep, deep. Then I bury my bone in the hole and cover it with dirt. There! Now no other dog can find it.

"Hurry up! Follow me!"

"No, not that way. What is wrong with you?"

Phew. I buried my bone just in time, because suddenly I hear a pack of dogs coming my way—and they sound like big dogs.

"Why are you always going the wrong way?" I hear one of the dogs bark.

Now I can see them. I was right. They're huge dogs. Saint Bernards. Four of them. Two girls and two boys. And they're all barking at the same time.

Well, they're all barking except one. She's crying. "I'm sorry," she  whimpers. "I didn't mean to get lost."

"I am sick of rescuing you, Lena," the biggest dog barks back at her. "Your job is to rescue two-legs. Not to *be* rescued."

"Who ever heard of a Saint Bernard getting lost on the ski slopes?" the other girl dog asks her.

"You were lucky we came by," the smaller boy dog tells her. "You could have gotten hurt."

"I'm sorry," Lena whimpers again.

"We've got rescue work to do," the biggest Saint Bernard says. "We're going back to the lodge. You stay here and do whatever it is you do while *we're* working."

I watch as the three mean Saint Bernards run off, leaving Lena just lying there with her head in her paws.

Sniffle, sniffle, sniffle. Lena is whimpering.

I feel bad for her. It doesn't feel good to have another dog make fun of you. I know, because Frankie makes fun of me sometimes.

"Hello," I say, trying to be kind.

"Hi," Lena says in a quiet voice. "Are you from around here?"

"No," I answer. "I'm from Josh's house. My name's Sparky."

"Oh," she says. "Hi, Sparky. I'm Lena."

"Where are we?" I ask her.

"Zermatt. A village in Switzerland." Lena gives me a funny look. "You're not lost are you? Because I'm not very good at helping lost dogs. Or lost two-legs, either."

"I'm not lost," I tell her. That's the truth. You can't be lost if you're not trying to get anywhere.

Chomp, chomp, chomp. My teeth start that chattering thing again. My whole body is *shakity, shake, shaking.* I'm really cold.

I just want to dig up my bone and go home so I can lie on the nice warm couch in my living room.

But before I do, I'll take one more lick of the cold, wet, white stuff on the ground. I'm thirsty. Oh, and there's a spot that looks just like the yummy shave ice in Hawaii! I open my mouth and stick out my tongue.

"No!" Lena shouts before I can get one good lick. "Don't lick the yellow snow!"

I jump back. "Why not?" I ask her.

"Because my brother Luca left that yellow stuff in the snow," she says. "I mean, he had to go, so he lifted his leg and . . ."

Oh. I get it. I definitely don't want to lick *that*. "Thanks. I was thirsty. And this cold white stuff tastes like the water in my water bowl."

"It's called snow," Lena tells me. "We've got plenty of it in Zermatt. It gets cold up here in the mountains. So water comes down as snow."

"What's a mountain?" I ask her. Then I frown. I hope Lena doesn't think I'm dumb because I don't know what a mountain is.

But Lena just smiles and points to some high snow-covered things growing out of the ground behind us. "Those are mountains. See that big one there? That's the Matterhorn. I got lost in the woods on that today. I get lost all the time."

Lena looks sad again. I'm not going to dig up my bone right now. Lena seems so sad and lonely. I'm going to stay here a little while longer and be her friend. Everybody needs a friend.

29

CHAPTER 3

The first thing I ask my new friend is, "Where can I find some food? I'm hungry."

"There is always leftover cheese and bread behind the lodge," Lena tells me.

Yummy, yum, yum! I love cheese. And bread. My tail starts to wag. It loves cheese and bread, too. Which is weird, since my tail doesn't have a mouth to eat with.

"Let's go to the lodge!" I bark excitedly. Then I stop barking. "Um . . . what's a lodge?"

"It's a building where two-legs eat, drink, and warm themselves," Lena explains. "Dogs can't go inside the lodge. But there's always food and water for us outside."

"You live *outside*?" I ask her. That sounds terrible. It's so cold here.

Lena shakes her head. "We have nice doghouses right near the lodge. That way we are always around if two-legs need rescuing." She stops for a minute and sighs. "My brothers and sister do the rescuing. I'm not good at finding my way around."

Grumble, grumble, rumble. That's my tummy telling me it's hungry. "Can we go to the lodge now?" I ask her.

"Okay," Lena agrees. But she doesn't move.

"Um . . . do you know where the lodge is?" I finally ask her.

Lena looks to her right. "I think it's that way," she says slowly. Then she shakes her head and looks to her left. "Or it could be that way. Or maybe behind us. Or . . ."

Lena's tail tucks itself between her legs, nervously. Then Lena starts to whimper.

Uh-oh. I have to help her. A good friend *always* tries to help. There has to be a way for us to get to the lodge. I just have to *thinkety, think, think* of something.

Wait a minute! My tail starts to wag excitedly. It knows I have an idea. A great idea!

"Didn't your brother say they were going to the lodge?" I ask Lena.

Lena nods. "Yes. My brothers and sister always wait there until it is time to go out on their next rescue."

"Well, there's yellow snow over here," I tell Lena as I use my snout to point to the right. "It wasn't there before. Neither were these three sets of paw prints. I bet they were left by your brothers and sister on their way back to the lodge."

"Maybe," Lena says. "It's worth a try."

Rumble, rumble, grumble. My tummy is talking to me again. It's really hungry. And so am I.

"Come on," I tell Lena. "Let's follow the yellow snow!"

CHAPTER 4

"Well, look who made it back," the biggest of Lena's brothers says as we arrive at the lodge. "I'm surprised we didn't have to come rescue you again."

"Cut it out, Luca," Lena's sister says. But she doesn't tell Lena that she did a good job getting back to the lodge.

Lena's other brother cocks his head and smiles a little. "It didn't take you very long at all this time," he tells her.

"Thanks, Jonas," Lena says.

Jonas seems a little nicer than Luca.

"Come on, Jonas and Charlotte," Luca says to Lena's brother and sister. "I smell bread in the bin around the corner."

Lena doesn't say anything when her brothers and sister go off without her to find the bread. But I can tell my new friend is sad. That makes me sad.

Just then, a two-leg dumps a few hunks of cheese into one of the food bowls.

I run over and take a big chunk of smelly, sour cheese in my mouth and bite down. *Yummy, yum, yum!*

"It's Swiss cheese," Lena explains.

"Boy, do I love cheese!"

"Me too," Lena says. "I'm glad you said to follow the yellow snow. How did you know to do that?"

"I don't know," I admit. "It just came to me."

Suddenly, out of the corner of my eye, I spot a tall, thin two-leg walking out of the lodge. He has dark fur on top of his head, like my Josh. He walks really fast on his two legs, like my Josh. And he has a long furry leash around his neck, like my Josh wears when it gets cold.

How did my Josh get all the way

to Zermatt? Does he have a magic bone, too?

"Josh! Josh! Josh!" I bark excitedly. I take off after him, forgetting all about Lena and the cheese.

"Sparky! Where are you going?" Lena calls out.

I don't answer her.

"Josh! Josh! Josh!" I bark again.

Josh doesn't turn around. So I keep following him.

Josh turns right. I turn right.

Josh turns left. I turn left.

41

Josh sits on a cold bench. I sit on a cold bench.

I look over and smile at Josh. He gives me a funny look and moves away from me on the bench.

I give him a funny look. Wait a minute. He's not *my* Josh.

Whoa! Suddenly the bench I'm sitting on starts to move. Before I know what's happening, the not-Josh and I fly up in the air.

"AAAAAHHHHH!" I yelp.

I look down. The not-Josh and I are flying high over the snow. Up over the lodge. High over the trees. I shut my eyes. I can't look.

Wiggle, waggle, gulp!

44

CHAPTER 5

"Let me down! Let me down!" I bark, as the not-Josh and I fly over the trees.

The not-Josh is shouting, too. I don't understand what he's saying. But I can tell he's not happy. In fact, the not-Josh is so not happy that if he had a tail, he would tuck in between his legs.

That's what my tail is doing right now. It's tucked so far under me, I don't know if it will ever come out.

"Let me down! Let me down!" I bark again.

The not-Josh shouts louder. So do some of the other two-legs flying high in the sky. None of us are happy up here.

Wiggle, waggle, wow! Our barking and shouting is working! We start to go down. The tops of the trees are higher than I am again.

Bump, thump, thump.

I leap off the bench and onto the snow. It's still cold and wet, but I don't care. I'm just happy to be on the ground.

I look down. Oops. There is a puddle of yellow snow at my feet. That kind of thing happens when I'm scared.

The not-Josh walks away from me as fast as he can. The other two-legs scramble to get away from me, too.

"Wait for me, not-Josh!" I call out. "Wait for me, other two-legs!"

But they don't wait. Now I'm all alone.

I don't like it here. I want to go back to the lodge where Lena is. But how? I don't want to have to be rescued by Lena's mean brothers and sister.

Wait a minute. I am thinking a really great *thinkety-think thought*! Some of these two-legs might be heading to the lodge! After all, that's where the food is. And two-legs like to eat just as much as dogs. If I follow the two-legs, I bet I'll find my way back to the lodge, Lena, and the Swiss cheese!

I walk over to a crowd of two legs and wait for them to start walking. But the two-legs just stand there.

48

I look down. Wow! Those two-legs have the weirdest paws I've ever seen. Their paws are long and skinny. And they don't have any toes or claws. I wonder if they can even walk with paws like that.

"Hello, two-legs. Are you going to the lodge?" I bark excitedly.

"Aaaah!"

I must have scared one of them. She screams and falls backward. And then, suddenly, her long, skinny, clawless paws pop off!

"Aaaah!" Now it's my turn to scream.

The two-leg hits another two-leg as she falls. That two-leg falls. And *his* paws pop off!

That two-leg knocks over a third two-leg. And his paws pop off, too! Suddenly, all around me, two-legs are falling to the ground. Their paws are popping off all over the place. And they're all shouting at the same time.

I don't blame them. I'd shout, too, if *my* paws popped off.

But the pawless two-legs are all shouting at *me*, like it's my fault. And it's not my fault. I never touched their long, skinny, clawless paws.

I don't like the shouting. And it's scary watching their paws pop off. I have to get out of here.

Suddenly, I spy some two-legs with regular-size paws. They aren't shouting. They're near a row of long, flat chew toys. The toys remind me of the long toy my friend Lolani stood on to ride the waves in Maui. But instead of standing on the toy, these two-legs are sitting.

I watch as a two-leg sits down and another two-leg pushes him toward the hill. *Whoosh!* The toy and the two-leg zip down the side of the hill.

I race over to another long wooden toy. Quickly, I push it to the edge of the hill with my nose. The toy starts to slide downhill. I leap on top of it.

Wiggle, waggle, whoosh! I'm sliding down the mountain. The wind is blowing my fur. My ears are pressed back against my head. My teeth are chattering as I *bumpity, bump, bump* down the hill.

I whoosh past a group of green trees. I whiz past a brown house with smoke coming out the top. I swish past three two-legs with no legs.

My tail tucks itself way, way under me. I don't blame it. I'd hide under me, too, if I could figure out how.

Swish! A two-leg with long skinny paws zooms past me. She's going even faster than I am. But she doesn't seem scared. What a brave two-leg!

Look! I'm nearing the bottom of the hill!

Thump, thump, bump! The fast-sliding toy throws me into the snow. The snow is cold and wet, but I'm sure glad it's soft.

Uh-oh! Another two-leg with long skinny paws is zooming right toward me. "Watch out!" I bark at him.

The two-leg moves around me. Then, *plop*! He is on the ground. And he's shouting at me. I don't know why. I didn't *make* him fall.

Shakity, shake, shake! I shake the snow from my fur.

"Sparky! There you are!" I hear Lena call. "Why did you leave?"

I don't want to tell Lena about following the not-Josh up in the air. It's too embarrassing. So instead I say, "I was exploring. But I'm back. And I'm still hungry. Let's get more cheese."

Lena shakes her head. "The cheese is all gone."

"All of it?" I ask her.

Lena nods. "But there is another place we can get some treats," she continues.

"Where? Where?" I ask. My tail starts wagging. My paws bounce up and down.

"A two-leg in town has a store filled with dog food, toys, and treats. He gives the treats to dogs to thank them for rescuing two-legs. He gives treats to me, too. Even though I never . . ." Lena's voice drifts off.

I know Lena is sad that she's never saved anyone. But I'm glad to hear that this nice two-leg gives treats to dogs who have never rescued anyone.

That means I'll get some! My tail wags harder. My paws bounce higher.

My mouth gets watery, and my tongue pops out. "I want treats!" I bark. "Let's go!"

CHAPTER 6

"I was sure the shop was right around that corner," Lena says. "I don't know how we missed it. Unless . . ."

"Unless what?" I ask her. Lena and I have been walking through the village for a long, long time. We've seen lots of horses and plenty of two-legs. But we haven't seen or sniffed a single dog treat.

"Unless we were supposed to turn left," Lena says. "Oh, I don't know. I usually follow Luca, Jonas, and

zermatt
1620m

Charlotte to the shop. I have no idea how to get there on my own. I have no idea how to get *anywhere* on my own. I don't even know where we are now."

"Come on, Lena," I say. "You have to recognize this place. You *live* in Zermatt. Look around."

Lena looks around. I look around.

"I think we have to go this way," Lena says finally. She doesn't sound very sure, but she starts walking uphill anyway.

We pass shops and houses. I smell something sweet coming from the trees and see smoke rising from the roofs of the houses. The smoke smells like it did at our house that time Josh let his bread turn black. He didn't eat that blackened bread. He just fed it to the round can in the kitchen.

Josh. The more I think about him, the more I miss him. The more I want to go back and take a big bite of my bone so I can go home.

But I don't think we're heading back to my bone. We keep walking higher and higher up a mountain. There's nothing here but snow. Lots and lots of snow. Some snow is lying flat on the ground. Some snow is sitting in the trees. And some of the snow is packed together into lumpy, bumpy balls.

But not little balls like Josh uses when we play fetch. Huge balls. Giant balls. Snowballs as big as houses!

Lena looks around. "How did we

wind up in Iglu-Dorf?" she wonders aloud.

Why is she asking me? I don't even know what Iglu-Dorf is. "How did we wind up *where*?" I ask.

"Iglu-Dorf," Lena repeats. "This village. It's made up of snow houses called *igloos*."

"Do two-legs live in these igloos?" I ask her. "The same way Josh and I live in our house?"

"I think the two-legs just visit," Lena says. "My brothers and sister have led me up here lots of times, and it's always different two-legs staying here. They sleep and eat inside the igloos, and when they leave, different two-legs come and sleep and eat inside them."

Eating and sleeping in a snow house? *Wiggle, waggle, weird.* Two-legs do the strangest things.

I walk around to get a better look at the snow houses. There's a hole in the giant snowball. A dog could wander right inside.

"AAAAAHHHHH!" A two-leg shouts as I walk inside the giant snowball.

"AAAHHHHH!" I bark back at the two-leg. Actually at the two-*legs*. There are a whole bunch of them inside the giant snowball.

Sniffety, sniff, sniff. It smells like they're eating something cheesy in here. I gotta have some!

I race over to a big pot of cheese. It's all gooey. *Mmmm.* I love gooey cheese.

The two legs start shouting. I don't think they want to share their cheese.

"No, Sparky! Don't lick the cheese fondue!" Lena warns. She doesn't want me to share the cheese, either.

But it is too late. My tongue is already sticking itself into the pot of gooey cheese.

"Owie, ow, ow, ow!" I shout. The cheese is hot. It burns my tongue. "Owie, ow, ow!"

I'm not the only one shouting. The two-legs are shouting, too. They are really angry that I tried to share their cheese.

That's okay. I don't want any more of that *hottie, hot, hot* cheese, anyway.

One of the two-legs waves his hands at me. He's trying to shoo me out of the igloo.

The shouting is loud. My tongue is hurting. My tail is scared. My paws start running toward the door. Fast. Faster. *Fastest.*

"Sparky, wait up!" Lena shouts. I can hear her breathing heavily as she runs after me. "Don't leave without me. Please. I don't want to be lost and all alone . . . again."

I stop for a minute. Lena sounds scared. Just like I am.

"Don't worry, Lena," I tell her. "I wouldn't leave you lost and all alone. I know exactly how you feel."

Lena shakes her head. "You can't understand how I feel. I'm a Saint Bernard. I was born to rescue people. But I always wind up getting lost and having to be rescued myself. It's embarrassing."

"I know what it feels like to be lost, because my magic . . ." I stop talking for moment. I don't know if I should tell Lena about my magic bone. What if she decides she wants to use it to get out of Zermatt and away from her brothers and sister? She might go find my bone and steal it.

No. That would never happen. Lena is too nice to steal my bone. And besides, she probably wouldn't be able to find it. I don't mean that in a mean way. It's just that she has a lot of trouble finding things.

"I have a magic bone," I explain. "When I take a bite out of it, there's a giant *kaboom*. And the next thing I know, I'm somewhere I've never been before. I don't know where I am or where to go. I have to depend on other dogs to help me."

Lena looks like she isn't sure whether or not to believe me. I don't blame her. A *kabooming* magic bone is pretty hard to believe in.

Finally she asks, "Where's your bone now?"

"Back where you first met me," I tell her. "Near the green trees and the two-leg with no legs. I buried it under the snow and dirt so it would be safe. I hope I can find my way there soon. I'm ready to go back to my house."

"You have your own house?" Lena asks me.

"I share it with my two-leg, Josh," I tell her. "He's really nice. He gives me kibble and scratches me behind the ears . . .

That's it!" I shout out excitedly.

Lena gives me a funny look. "*What's* it?"

"You can come live with Josh and

me," I say. "You and I will find my bone. Then we'll take a bite at the exact same time. We can *kaboom* back to my house together."

"Would Josh want another dog?" Lena asks me.

I nod, "Josh loves dogs. We have lots of room in our house. And our yard is big. But not so big that you could get lost," I add quickly.

Lena cocks her head to one side. I can tell she is thinking. "I would like that," she says finally.

"Great!" I say. "Come on, Lena. Let's go. We have a magic bone to find."

CHAPTER 7

"Are you sure we're going the right way?" I ask Lena.

I'm so tired. Lena and I have been walking for a long time. But we still haven't found the two-leg with no legs who is standing near my bone.

"I hope so," Lena says. "I don't really know," she admits.

My heart starts *thumpety, thump, thumping*. It doesn't like being lost.

Suddenly, my ears perk up. I hear something.

"Two-legs!" I bark. "Lots of them.

Just like at the lodge."

"I hear them, too," Lena barks back.

"Maybe if we follow the two-legs, we'll get back to the lodge," I tell Lena. "And once we're there we can hopefully find the place where I buried my bone."

My paws start running toward the sound of two-legs talking. "Wait for us, two-legs!" I bark to them.

A minute later, Lena and I are right in the middle of a big group of two-legs' legs. All we can see are two-leg knees and two-leg feet.

"I don't think this is the lodge, Sparky," Lena says.

I don't think so, either. The lodge smells like cheese, bread, and sweet trees. But this place doesn't smell like food or trees. And the lodge . . .

Wiggle, waggle, uh-oh!

The lodge is on the ground. But we're not on the ground anymore. We're sitting in a metal machine, kind of like the one Josh drives. Only this metal machine doesn't have four round paws. And it isn't in the street. It's flying in the sky.

I don't like it up in the sky.

"Let me out of here!" I bark.

The two-legs all move away from me. They all seem to be talking at once. I can't understand what they're saying, but they sound scared. I don't know why. I'm not scary Neither is Lena.

I can tell that the two-legs don't want us here. But they don't open a door to let us out of the metal machine.

At least not at first. But a few minutes later, the door to the machine opens. I wiggle my way through the two-leg legs and out into the cold air.

Wiggle, waggle, wahoo! I feel snow on my paws. I bend down and give it a big lick. "I love you, snow. I love you!" I bark happily.

76

Lena pads her way over to me. "I've never seen this place before," she tells me. "This is the most lost I've ever been."

I'm not so happy anymore.

My ears perk up again. I hear a two-leg shouting. My eyes open wide. There's a two-leg running right for Lena and me.

My tail slips between my legs.

My heart starts *thumpety, thump, thumping.* That two-leg looks like he's trying to catch us. I don't like when two-legs try to catch me. The last time a two-leg caught me, he threw me into the back of a metal machine with four round paws and drove me straight to the pound in London! I don't see any metal machines here. Which means this two-leg probably isn't a dogcatcher. But I'm not taking any chances!

"Come on, Lena," I bark. "We've gotta get out of here!"

My paws start running. Fast. Faster. *Whoops!* I slide across the ground on my rear end. Wow! That's cold.

Slam! Lena slides right into me.

Lena and I crash into the knees of the two-legs around us. They fall to the ground and slide into the walls. Then they start shouting.

But Lena and I don't stop to listen to their shouting. We hop back up on our four legs and keep running. We can't let that dogcatcher catch us!

"It's r-r-really c-c-c-cold in here," I say through my chattering teeth.

"Glaciers are cold," Lena says. "I think we're inside Glacier Palace."

"You think?" I ask her. "Don't you *know*?"

"I heard Charlotte talking about Glacier Palace once," Lena says. "She rescued some two-legs who got stuck up here during a snowstorm. She said it was cold and slippery and all made of ice."

That sure sounds like where Lena and I are right now. The walls and the ground are all made of slippery, cold ice.

"Look," I say, pointing my snout toward a horse and some funny-looking birds. "Those are statues," I tell Lena. I know all about statues. I saw a lot of them in Rome. But these statues are different. I can see right through them.

Lena runs on ahead. I start to follow her. But then I stop. I want to get a closer look at these statues. It will only take a minute. And they are so pretty.

The statues are different than the ones I saw in Rome. They're cold. Really, really cold.

I walk over and sniff the horse statue's butt—just to say hello. *Sniffety, sniff, uh-oh!* My nose! It's stuck! To the icy statue's butt!

Just then I hear footsteps coming up behind me. *Two-leg* footsteps!

I try to pull my nose off the horse statue's butt. But it's still stuck. *Ouch!*

And the footsteps are still coming. I know I should run. But I can't.

I want to bark out for Lena. But I can't do that, either. If I bark, the two-leg—who might or might not be a dogcatcher—will know I'm here for sure.

I'm trapped. What can I do?

Be a statue, I thinkety think. *Don't move.*

It's not the best plan. I'm not see-through like the other statues. And I'm not cold like them, either. But it's the only plan I've got.

My tail wags nervously.

"Stop moving," I whisper to my tail. My tail stops wagging.

My heart is *thumpety, thump, thumping*.

"Stop thumping," I whisper to my

heart. But it keeps thumping. I hope the two-leg doesn't hear it.

The two-leg is getting closer. I hear his footsteps. But I stop my eyes from looking for him. I'm a statue. Statue eyes don't move. No part of me moves. Not even to breathe.

The two-leg comes closer. And closer. And closer. And then . . . *he runs right past me.*

I let out a long breath. My breath is hot. I can see it in the air. I wiggle my nose. *Wiggle, waggle, whoopee!* My hot breath helped my nose break free!

My paws start running down the icy hallway! It doesn't take me long to catch up to Lena.

"We have to get away from here!" I tell her.

"I know," Lena agrees. "Only I don't know which way is out of here."

"Come on," I say. I start running through the slippery tunnel. Only this time we're running out, not in. "Run toward the sunlight. The sun only shines outside."

Lena and I run and run. We hurry through the snow, past trees and rocks. I don't know where we're going. I don't even care. I just want to get away from the two-legs. I don't know which ones I can trust and which ones I can't. And the last thing I want to do is run into a two-leg who will put Lena and me in the pound.

But Lena and I aren't alone. I can hear sounds coming from behind a big clump of trees nearby.

"Wait. Lena, stop!" I bark to her. "Do you hear that?"

Lena stops. Her ears perk up. "What?"

"That rustling noise," I say. "There's something in those trees."

"Let's get out of here," Lena tells me.

I know she is right. It could be another dogcatcher. Or a big bully dog who will be mean to us.

Now I can hear whimpering. Dogcatchers don't whimper. And neither do bullies.

Slowly, I pad over to the trees. I peek around the corner. And then I see them. They're all alone, shaking and whimpering.

"Lena!" I shout. "Hurry! I found some two-legs who need your help!"

CHAPTER 8

"Oh no," Lena tells me. "I won't. I can't!"

"Lena, you *have* to rescue them," I insist. "It's your job."

The two-legs are still whimpering. One of them has water dripping from her eyes. She's sitting on a log, holding one of her paws.

"You can do this," I tell Lena. "You can get them back to the lodge."

Lena shakes her head. "I can't," she tells me.

But I won't let her give up. Not now.

Snow has started to fall from the sky. And not just a little. There's lots and lots of snow coming down. It's already making it hard to see. If we don't move now, we may never find our way back!

"Come on, Lena," I say. "You have to find the lodge. I'll help you."

"How?" Lena asks.

Good question.

I look around. Suddenly, I spy a brown house with smoke coming out of the top. I've seen a house like that house before—when I was whizzing down the hill that led to the lodge.

"The lodge is at the bottom of a big hill, right?" I ask Lena.

Lena nods.

"Then we have to go down," I say. "Come on."

Lena and I start to walk downhill. But I realize the two-legs aren't following us. The one holding her paw doesn't even stand up. I don't think she can.

How are we going to get her down the hill?

Thinkety, think, think. I look around. And that's when I see one of those long, wooden, fast-sliding toys. The two-leg can sit on the toy. We will pull her down the hill.

I use my nose to push the sliding toy closer to her.

The two-leg stares at me. But she doesn't move. The snow is getting thicker and thicker. We have to hurry.

"Come on, Hurt Two-Leg," I bark at her. "Climb on."

Hurt Two-Leg doesn't do anything. But the other two-leg bends down and helps her onto the sliding snow toy.

"Okay," I tell Lena. "You have to pull her. I'm not big or strong enough."

"I can do it," Lena says. She takes the rope at the front of the sliding snow toy in her mouth.

"Now sniff," I tell Lena. "Does anything smell like something you've smelled before?"

Lena sniffs and sniffs and sniffs. "I smell trees. And maybe cheese."

"There are trees and cheese at the lodge," I say.

"And bread," Lena says. "I smell bread. We're getting closer," she adds

as she pulls Hurt Two-Leg through the snow.

The other two-leg follows close behind us.

The snow is really coming down now. We are the only ones on the mountain. There are no two-legs or dogs anywhere. Already the snow is covering up some of the smells on the mountain. And soon we won't be able to see.

"Hurry, Lena, hurry!" I bark to her.

"Look! I know that snowman with the carrot for his nose," Lena says, pointing to a group of two-legs with no legs. "I've seen it before."

A carrot. *Yummy, yum, yum.* I love carrots. But there's no time to stop now. I have to follow Lena and get these two-legs to safety. Lena sounds like she knows where she's going now. At least I hope she does.

Whoosh, whoosh, whoosh. The wind is blowing even harder now. Snow is flying into my eyes and my ears. It's cold and wet out here. But we can't stop. Not now.

The two-legs don't look so scared now. They think Lena knows where she's going. I hope they're right.

"Look!" Lena barks excitedly to me. "That's where I met you!"

I'm excited, too. Through the trees I see a round, snowy two-leg with no legs. I know that my magic bone is buried right near him! And the lodge isn't far from there, either—just a trail of yellow snow and some paw-print paths away.

Lena's ears perk up. "I hear lots of two-legs talking," she says.

I hear the two-legs, too.

"Come on, Lena!" I bark. "We're near the lodge!"

Lena and I turn away from the tree and the snowy two-leg with no legs and head to the lodge. It's impossible to see Jonas's, Charlotte's, and Luca's paw prints now because of the fresh snow that's fallen. But I can still smell the yellow snow. So I follow the scent of the yellow snow.

And then I see the lodge! Lena and I have gotten the two-legs back safely. Our job is done!

"Come on, Lena," I bark to her. "Let's go back to the two-leg with no legs who stands by the tree. We can dig up my bone and *kaboom* home together."

But Lena doesn't follow me. She can't. She's surrounded by two-legs. They've all come running to greet Lena and the two-legs who were lost in the woods.

I watch as Luca, Charlotte, and Jonas race over to Lena.

"*You* rescued the two-legs?" Luca asks her.

"Sure!" Lena replies. "Isn't that what Saint Bernards do?"

"Yeah, but you never . . . ," Luca starts. "I mean how did *you* . . . ?"

Lena doesn't let him finish. "I followed my nose," she says. "And my eyes and my ears."

"You're a hero," Jonas tells her.

"No one even knew those two-legs were lost out there."

"Come back to the lodge and have some cheese, Lena," Charlotte says. "You've earned it."

"Okay," Lena agrees. But before she leaves with her brothers and sister, Lena looks over and smiles at me.

"Thanks, Sparky," she barks.

"You're a good rescue dog," I tell her.

"So are you," she barks back.

I smile. I helped Lena lead the two-legs back to the lodge. And I'm glad I did. Because now Lena knows what to do, too.

I'm not sad that Lena doesn't want to come home with me anymore. It's okay. Saint Bernard rescue dogs belong in Switzerland. Just like I belong home with Josh.

It's hard to see with all the snow flying. But I follow my own paw prints back to the two-leg with no legs that stands near the sweet-smelling tree. I start *diggety, dig, digging* a hole. Dirt and snow fly all over the place. And then I see it. My magic bone is right where I left it.

But wait! There's something else
nearby. A shoe. The kind of shoe two-
legs wear when it's cold and snowy. I
bet Josh would like that shoe. I grab
the shoe and hold it tight in my paws.
And then . . . *chomp*. I bite down on
my bone.

Wiggle, waggle, whew. I feel dizzy—like my insides are spinning all around—but my outsides are standing still. Stars are twinkling in front of my eyes—even though it's daytime! All around me I smell food—fried chicken, salmon, roast beef. But there isn't any food in sight.

Kaboom! Kaboom! Kaboom!

A minute later, the *kabooming* stops.

I look around. There's my tree. My fence. My house. I'm home!

I'd better hide my bone before anyone sees it. Quickly, I *diggety, dig, dig* through the snow and into the hard dirt by the flowerbed that has no flowers. I drop my bone in the deep hole and bury it.

Just then, I hear something outside the yard. It's a big metal machine—the kind with four round paws. Josh is home!

Josh! Josh! Josh! My paws race to him. Fast. Faster. *Fastest!*

My fur falls down and covers my eyes. I can't see where I'm running. But my paws keep going. Fast. Faster. *Boom!*

I slam *right into* Josh! He falls
into the cold, wet snow. Boy, does he
look surprised.

Josh spots my ripped coat and
booties lying in the snow. Uh-oh. He
looks kind of angry.

Then Josh sees the shoe I brought him. Now he looks confused.

I wish I could tell Josh all about the igloos, the ice statues, and the hot and cold cheeses in Zermatt. But I can't. So I just lick his cheek.

Josh smiles. He isn't surprised or angry or confused anymore. He's happy.

So am I.

I follow Josh into our house. He pours some kibble into my bowl.

Sniffety, sniff, sniff. My kibble doesn't smell as good as the cheese in Switzerland. But that's okay. It's warm and dry in my house. I know where everything is. I don't need anyone to rescue me now. I'm home. And that's *wiggle, waggle, wonderful*!

Fun Facts about Sparky's Adventures in Switzerland:

The Matterhorn

The Matterhorn is a mountain that sits in the Alps between Switzerland and Italy. It is not the highest mountain in the Swiss Alps, but it is likely the most photographed mountain in the world. Many people consider it the symbol of Switzerland.

Zermatt

One of the first things a visitor to this Swiss village will notice is that there are no cars. Most people travel on foot, though there are horse-drawn carriages and electro-mobiles to help visitors get around. Zermatt has shops, restaurants, ski schools, and working dairy farms.

Iglu-Dorf

This igloo village in Zermatt is actually a hotel. Visitors stay warm and dry in sleeping bags when they spend the night in the igloos built from blocks of frozen snow. Guests can eat fondue, which is small pieces of bread dipped into hot melted cheese.

Glacier Palace

Zermatt's Glacier Palace is the highest glacier palace in the world. The only way for visitors to reach it is by one of the two cable cars that lead up to the glacier. Guests enter the palace through an underground ice tunnel and then walk through the icy palace. Artists use actual glacier ice to build ice sculptures of cold-weather animals like reindeer, horses, and penguins.

MAGIC BONE

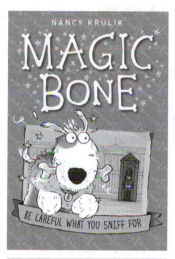

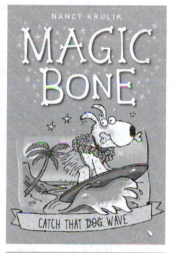

About the Author

Nancy Krulik is the author of more than 200 books for children and young adults, including three *New York Times* best sellers. She is best known for being the author and creator of several successful book series for children, including Katie Kazoo, Switcheroo; How I Survived Middle School; and George Brown, Class Clown. Nancy lives in Manhattan with her husband, composer Daniel Burwasser, and her crazy beagle mix, Josie, who manages to drag her along on many exciting adventures without ever leaving Central Park.

About the Illustrator

You could fill a whole attic with Seb's drawings! His collection includes some very early pieces made when he was four—there is even a series of drawings he did at the movies in the dark! When he isn't doodling, he likes to make toys and sculptures, as well as bows and arrows for his two boys, Oscar and Leo, and their numerous friends. Seb is French and lives in England. His website is www.sebastienbraun.com.